James Mayhew
presents

Ella Bella
BALLERINA
~ and ~

A Midsummer Night's Dream

For Raffi Bowen
~ fairy, ballerina and shooting star !
J. M.

ORCHARD BOOKS
First published in Great Britain in 2015 by The Watts Publishing Group
This edition first published in 2016
3 5 7 9 10 8 6 4 2
Text and illustrations © James Mayhew, 2015

A CIP catalogue record for this book is available from the British Library.
ISBN 978 1 40832 644 2
Printed and bound in China

MIX
Paper from
responsible sources
FSC® C104740

FSC
www.fsc.org

Orchard Books
An imprint of Hachette Children's Group
Part of The Watts Publishing Group Limited
Carmelite House
50 Victoria Embankment
London EC4Y 0DZ
An Hachette UK Company
www.hachette.co.uk
www.hachettechildrens.co.uk

James Mayhew
presents

Ella Bella
BALLERINA
~ and ~

A Midsummer Night's Dream

ORCHARD

Ella Bella and her friends were at the old
theatre, getting ready for their ballet class.
"Today, my darlings, you can try on some
costumes," said their teacher, Madame Rosa.

Everyone tried on something different.
Ella Bella chose a fairy costume with little
purple flowers.
"You all look wonderful," said Madame Rosa.
"Now we need some music!"

Madame Rosa opened her magical music box and out poured a shimmering tune. "This is *A Midsummer Night's Dream* by Felix Mendelssohn," she said. "It's based on Shakespeare's story about fairies. There is even a fairy king and queen!"

"It does sound just like fairy music,"
said Ella Bella, dreamily.
"Let's all dance like fairies and elves!"
said Madame Rosa.

The children danced to the music,
waving their arms and twirling around.
"Enchanting, my dears," said Madame Rosa.

All too soon the lesson was over, and the children went to get changed . . . except Ella Bella.

She wanted to have one more dance in her fairy flower costume, as it was so beautiful.

Ella Bella opened the lid of
the musical box. As the fairy tune
played, she began to dance.

"Pssst!" someone called.
Ella Bella saw an elf smiling at her.
"May I borrow those flowers in your hair?
I have searched the world over for them."

"My name is Puck," said the elf. "Oberon,
King of Fairyland, needs those flowers to
win back the heart of Titania, his fairy queen.
It seems she no longer loves him . . . instead
she spends all her days playing with fairies
and elves."

"What will the flowers do?" asked Ella Bella.
"They are magic flowers, and they will help
with some midsummer mischief!" said Puck.
"Now, take my hand, fairy child! Oberon awaits!"

Ella Bella realised they were flying high above
a forest. It was a warm summer night and the
sky shimmered with stars. The moon covered
the trees in a silvery light, as fairies flitted
around like fireflies and moths.

Ella Bella and Puck landed beside
a great old oak tree where Oberon,
King of Fairyland, was waiting.

"I found the magic flowers," said Puck.
"Well done," said Oberon. "They are called
Love in Idleness. I will use them to cast a
midsummer spell on Queen Titania."

"How will the spell work?" asked Ella Bella,
with a curtsey.
"Titania will fall in love with the first creature
she sees," laughed Oberon. "I hope it will be
a very silly kind of beast! Perhaps then she
will remember that I am her true love."

"Come on," said Puck. "Let's find someone really funny for the fairy queen to fall in love with!"

They giggled and tiptoed off between the trees.

In a clearing, some friends were practising a play.

A man called Bottom was reading the script,
but he kept getting the words wrong.
"Oh dear," he said. "I must practise more,
or I shall make a fool of myself!"

"Let's play a trick on Bottom," said Puck. "He reminds me of a silly donkey!"

Puck sprinkled some magic on Bottom, and he began to change . . .

He grew longs ears and a furry snout!

Bottom had no idea he looked so funny
and wondered why his friends all ran away!
He set off into the woods after them.

"Now he is the perfect love for our
queen!" giggled Puck.

Bottom found a grove filled with flowers. There slept the beautiful fairy queen, Titania. She was surrounded by fairies singing.

Lulla Lulla Lullaby

Oberon had already put the magic
flower juice upon Titania's eyes.
Then, Bottom tried singing too . . .

Titania awoke to Bottom's braying. "Oh, my lovely!" she said, as she stroked Bottom's ears and gazed into his eyes. It was quite clear that Titania was in love with him!

They danced under the moon, and then, at last, fell asleep in each other's arms.

"They look so silly!" giggled Ella Bella and Puck. Oberon appeared. "Yes, and when Titania awakes she will hope this donkey was only a midsummer dream," he smiled. "Now, remove the spell from the foolish Bottom."

Puck waved his hands, and Bottom's donkey ears vanished, and his own face was restored. He ran off to find his friends.

Already the moon was fading and the sky was growing pale. When Titania awoke, she saw Oberon and smiled.

"Oh, my dearest king, I am so glad to see you," she said. "I dreamed I was in love with a donkey!"

"My queen," said Oberon. "Will you stay with me always?"

"Always, my love," said Titania.

Midsummer Night was over and everything was back as it should be. "And now, farewell, fairy Ella Bella!" said Puck. "And thank you!" Ella Bella waved as he flew off into the sky like a shooting star!

The music stopped and Ella Bella saw she
was back in the old theatre. There on the
floor were the magic flowers. She carefully
picked them up.

Madame Rosa came to see how she was getting on.
"Here you are," said Ella Bella, handing her
the flowers.

"Thank you," said Madame Rosa. "Now, hurry out
of your costume. Your mamma is waiting and it will
soon be dark, and that's fairy time!"

On the way home with Mamma,
Ella Bella looked up at the sky
and saw the moon.

Suddenly, a shooting star flew across the sky.
She smiled as she thought of the fairy king
and queen, and her new friend Puck.

A Midsummer Night's Dream was first written
hundreds of years ago, by the most famous writer of all time,
William Shakespeare. In his play, there are many other characters,
including a rich duke and two young couples, falling in love, but the
best-loved characters have always been the magical fairy folk, and
their king and queen, Oberon and Titania.

The fairies in the play have delightful names like Cobweb, and
Peaseblossom. And the magical flower 'Love in Idleness' is a real
plant, it's a small wild pansy.

The enchanting music was written by Felix Mendelssohn to go with
the play. He started writing it when he was just 17 years old, and it is
full of sparkling and scurrying sounds to help us imagine the silvery
moonlight and fluttering fairy wings. You can even hear the sound of
Bottom, braying like a donkey!

The music for *A Midsummer Night's Dream* has
been used for ballets many times. The adventures
of the magical fairies in the moonlit forest is always
lots of fun, and the scenery and costumes are
wonderful to see.

If you could dress up as a magical elf or woodland fairy,
what would your costume be like?

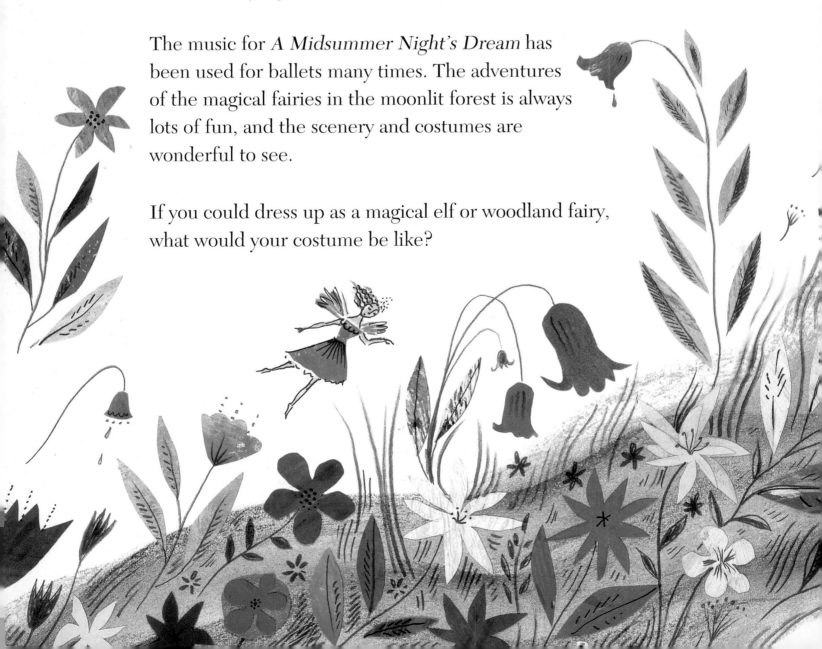